Mary Praises God

Mary Visits Elizabeth

Let's Light the Advent Candles

A Visit from St. Nicholas

Let's Read About Jesus

Christmas Cards Tell the Good News

His Star Still Shines for Us!

Let's Hang Our Stockings!

Christmas Treats to Share

Joy to the World

Mary and Joseph Go to Bethlehem

A Christmas Play

Jesus Is Born

Shepherds Hear the Angel's Message

Good News of Great Joy

Shepherds Visit Jesus

Shepherds Tell of Jesus' Birth

Christmas Surprises!

Christmas Visits with Family

Follow His Star

Christmas at Our House

Draw a picture of your family celebrating Christmas.

by _____

Gifts for Jesus